Juliet *nearly a* Vet

Rainforest Camp

Puffin Books

Juliet
nearly a
Vet

Rainforest Camp

REBECCA JOHNSON

Illustrated by Kyla May

Puffin Books

For Sharon Millar,
who dedicated her life to children.
X R

PUFFIN BOOKS

UK | USA | Canada | Ireland | Australia
India | New Zealand | South Africa | China

Penguin Books is part of the Penguin Random House group of companies
whose addresses can be found at global.penguinrandomhouse.com.

Penguin
Random House
PENGUIN BOOKS

First published by Penguin Random House Australia Pty Ltd, 2016

Cover and text design by Karen Scott © Penguin Random House Australia Pty Ltd
Typeset in New Century Schoolbook
Colour separation by Splitting Image Colour Studio, Clayton, Victoria
Printed and bound in Australia by Griffin Press, an accredited ISO AS/NZS 14001
Environmental Management Systems printer.

National Library of Australia
Cataloguing-in-Publication data:

Johnson, Rebecca.
Rainforest camp / Rebecca Johnson; illustrated by Kyla May.

ISBN: 978 0 14 350704 8 (pbk)
A823.4

MIX
Paper from
responsible sources
FSC® C009448

penguin.com.au

Hi! I'm Juliet. I'm ten years old.
And I'm nearly a vet!

I bet you're wondering how someone who is only ten
could nearly be a vet. It's pretty simple really.
My mum's a vet. I watch what she does and
I help out all the time. There's really not that
much to it, you know…

CHAPTER 1

Vets need to manage people as well

'Are you ready, Juliet?' Dad calls from the kitchen. 'The note says they want you at school by 8 o'clock.'

'Just about, Dad,' I say brightly, as I look down at my PJs and bulging suitcase and pull a face that makes Chelsea laugh.

I throw on my clothes and we are out the door and off down the road in no time at all.

Mrs Hodby marks our names off the roll. We are all so excited to be going on school camp in a rainforest and are talking and laughing so much we can hardly hear each other over the noise in the bus.

Portia and Tiffany are the last to arrive. When they get on, everyone goes quiet for a moment. They're dressed like they are going to a fancy dinner out somewhere.

'Look at all their jewellery!' whispers Chelsea.

Mrs Hodby doesn't look too happy. 'Hurry up and find a seat, girls. I hope you've got more sensible shoes than those for our bushwalks, or you are going to end up with very sore feet.'

All of the spare seats are singles.

Portia walks halfway down the aisle and whispers something to Maisy, and she jumps up and moves to the seat behind her so the two of them can sit together.

Chelsea and I look at each other and shake our heads.

We wave goodbye to our parents and head off. This is going to be the best three nights ever.

It takes a while to get there, and Mr Thomson, one of the teachers, has the whole bus singing songs about one hundred green bottles hanging on a wall and stuff. We all complain a bit at first, but really it is fun.

When we finally arrive, we pile out

of the bus and collect our bags. Mine is way bigger than Chelsea's and Maisy's, but they know why and help me lift it down.

'What's in the case?' says a voice behind me.

I know straight away who it is. I turn around to face Portia, but don't answer.

'Well, I know it isn't going to be clothes!' she sniggers as she looks me up and down.

Maisy, Chelsea and I just laugh and pretend she's said something funny. That's the thing about mean people. If you don't let them get to you, they usually move on pretty quickly.

We all walk down to the cabins and look for our names on the lists on the doors, to see which one we are in.

We are in the 'Cassowary Cabin'. The three of us get to be together, so we're really excited. Unfortunately, Portia and Tiffany are in our cabin too.

The three of us put our cases on the beds in the corner, leaving the other two spare across the room near the door.

It takes longer for Portia and Tiffany to get down to the cabin because their sandals keep slipping on the damp paths. Mrs Hodby did tell us to wear sneakers.

When Portia and Tiffany arrive,

they are very unhappy about the
sleeping arrangements.

'I don't like sleeping near the door,'
says Portia. 'Maisy, you need to swap
beds with me.'

Maisy actually starts to move her
things.

'Hang on,' I say. 'Where do you want
to sleep, Maisy?'

Maisy points to the bed she has
already put her gear on.

'Well, I want you to move,' says
Portia in a nasty voice.

'I can't believe you actually talk to
people like that,' I say, looking her in
the eye. Then I turn away and smile
at my friends. 'Leave your stuff there,

Maisy. Let's go and see what there is to do.'

I unzip my case and slide my vet kit under the end of my bed.

Portia sees it and points at it laughing. 'I knew it!' she sneers. 'I just knew Juliet the Vet would have to bring her little vet kit. What a joke!'

Tiffany laughs along nervously.

Chelsea is about to say something, but I stop her.

'Let's go and explore,' I say with a smile.

CHAPTER 2

Vets know how to protect animals from people

Mrs Hodby lets us all have a good look around before lunch. For each meal, a different group of kids has to help in the kitchen. Our turn is breakfast tomorrow. It is going to be fun making breakfast for fifty people ... I think!

We go and visit some other kids from our class and check out their cabins, then we look around the rest of the camping site. I love this place. There are birds everywhere, even large peacocks, and some very cheeky looking kookaburras hanging around the barbeque where Mr Thomson is cooking sausages for lunch.

There's a campfire set up for tonight, a high ropes course, a flying fox and a beautiful, clear creek. Paths lead away in all directions into the darkness of the rainforest.

'Is it tonight we go spotlighting for possums and things?' asks Maisy.

Chelsea pulls a neatly folded piece of paper from her back pocket. It's a list of all our activities. 'No,' she says, pointing at the form. 'Today it's the rainforest waterfall walk and a sing-a-long around the campfire. Tomorrow night is spotlighting and the glow-worm caves.'

Some kids have already set up a game of soccer. I hear them yelling and look over to see a brush turkey charging at their ball. They all laugh as the turkey attacks the ball.

Then I see why.

'It's got a mound!' I say, and we race towards them. Some of the boys are running at the turkey to stir it up even more. I try to explain and it's lucky I have my Vet Diary in my pocket. I already have a page on brush turkeys.

'Stop! He's got a mound with eggs buried in it!' I pant when we get there. 'He'll hurt himself trying to defend it from the ball.'

The boys stop what they are doing and come over to look at my notes.

I show them my diagram of a turkey nest. 'He's not playing a game,' I say. 'He's trying to stop the female's eggs from being damaged.'

Luckily everyone is actually quite interested in my diagram and they listen to what I have to say.

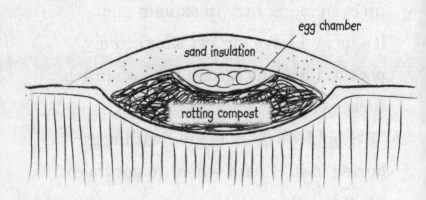

'That is a big nest for one bird!' says Patrick. 'I'm glad I'm not a turkey!'

'You kind of are,' laughs Cameron.

We inspect the size of the mound and I point out just how far out the nest reaches.

'Do you think you could have your

goals over there?' suggests Chelsea, pointing to a space a bit further away.

'I don't see why not,' says Sam. 'The turkey was probably their best player, anyway.' They happily switch their game around.

Suddenly we hear a shriek from the girls' toilets.

'What now?' asks Maisy, and we run over to look. There are girls running into the toilet and shower block, screaming, and then running out again.

Mrs Hodby is also making a beeline for the building. 'Girls,' she says, 'stop the yelling. What's going on?'

'There are toads in the shower!'

Chelsea, Maisy and I go in to have

a look. There are two very frightened-looking small brown frogs huddled in the corner of one shower cubicle, as well as a large Green Tree Frog high on the wall behind a pipe.

'They're not toads,' I say, pointing at the brown frogs. 'They're Striped Marsh Frogs. They would have come in here because it's dark and wet. I can put them outside if you like?'

'Um, I'm not sure,' says Mrs Hodby. 'Would you be able to do it without them getting hurt?'

'Of course she can!' laughs Chelsea. 'She's nearly a vet, Mrs Hodby.'

Mrs Hodby nods, but doesn't look completely convinced.

I wet my hands and carefully place my hands over both the frightened frogs. I can feel them jumping around between my fingers, trying to get out, but I hold still for a minute until they relax.

Then I scoop them up and cup my hands around them. Chelsea and Maisy clear the way for me to come out.

'Yuuuck!' shrieks Portia. 'Juliet is holding toads!'

A few other girls make gasping sounds as I walk around to the back of the shower block. It's cool and damp there, and there are some nice rocks for the frogs to hide in. I bend down and let them go.

'Well done, Juliet!' says Mrs Hodby.
She seems very glad that the screaming
has stopped.

'The Green Tree Frog will stay up
there and out of the way, I think,' I say.

'I agree,' says Mrs Hodby. 'We are
on a rainforest camp,' she says loudly
to all of the girls gathering around.
'We are here to experience nature in

the rainforest, so I don't want to hear any more carrying on about a few little frogs in the shower.'

We scoff our sausages in bread, throw a few little pieces to the chubby kookaburras and then race back to our cabins for hats, sunscreen and water bottles. Mrs Hodby reminds us to wear thick socks inside our sneakers and to tuck our pants into the socks.

'I'm not wearing my pants tucked in,' says Portia as we get organised. 'It looks ridiculous! It's bad enough wearing sneakers. I much prefer sandals.'

I see that Tiffany already has her pants tucked in, but she quickly pulls them out again.

I'm ready before everyone else, so
I start a quick list in my Vet Diary of
the animals we have seen so far.

RAINFOREST ANIMALS:

- Kookaburras
- Peacocks
- Brush turkey
- Striped Marsh Frogs
- Green Tree Frog

CHAPTER
3

Vets love exploring new places

We head off on our walk through the
rainforest. Mr Thomson is up the
front with one of the camp guides, and
Mrs Hodby is down the back, making
sure no one gets left behind.

Even though they all tell us to be
quiet and walk slowly so that we see
more animals, most kids seem to want
to charge along the tracks. We sound
like a travelling circus.

My friends and I are much happier
walking along with Mrs Hodby.

We drop back a little to hear the sounds of the rainforest around us.

'Look at that!' gasps Chelsea quietly, pointing to her left.

We all look over and see the most beautiful butterfly bobbing through the trees. Its large blue wings flash brightly whenever they catch the

sunlight that's breaking through the trees. We all stand quietly and watch it for ages. I don't think I have ever seen such a big butterfly. I try to memorise every part of it, so that I can look it up when I get home.

'Girls,' says Mrs Hodby. 'Look, there, through the trees. Can you see it?'

Chelsea is the first to see what she is pointing at.

'A kangaroo!' she whispers.

'It's got a joey!' breathes Maisy, just loudly enough for us all to hear. 'It's so cute.'

'I think it's a wallaby,' I whisper.

'How can you tell?' asks Mrs Hodby, surprised.

I whip out my diary from my back pocket.

'I have a whole section on kangaroos and wallabies, because we have them in the surgery sometimes,' I say.

I show them my table.

'You do know a LOT about animals, Juliet,' Mrs Hodby smiles.

KANGAROOS	WALLABIES
• Large • Eat grass • Long oversized legs • Dull one-coloured coat	• Small • Eat leaves • Short compact legs • Shiny coat with bright streaks

We spend all afternoon exploring the rainforest tracks, and end up at a beautiful waterfall. We're allowed to take our shoes and socks off and sit on the rocks and let our feet soak in the cool, clear water.

You can easily tell which socks belong to Portia and Tiffany. They have thin pretty socks with flowers and hearts all over them. Mine look like football socks next to theirs!

Mr Thomson brings around some biscuits and cake for us to eat while we relax and listen to the water falling down from the rocks above.

As I peer down into the clear water at my feet, I wonder what animals might be quietly staring up at me. I love the feeling of being out in the rainforest. The air smells so clean, and we are surrounded by greens of every shade. Animals are lucky to live here.

I turn over a small piece of bark on the ground and watch a shiny black beetle scurry for cover. There must be millions and millions of insects here, before you even start to count the other animals.

This is only the first afternoon of our camp, and we've already had a great time.

As it starts to cool down we head back to camp. We see more wallabies bounding through the undergrowth as we weave our way back.

We come out on a different path to the one we came in on. The camp guide, Alex, stops us all and points up. There are big, thick ropes pulled tightly between the trees.

'This is the high ropes course,' he says. 'Tomorrow your groups will all have a turn at climbing on these ropes to get from tree to tree.'

Everyone is talking at once. They

all seem super excited about it. I'm not so sure. I'm not really into high things.

'I can't wait!' says Maisy.

'Me either!' says Chelsea.

I'm trying to work out how you get up into the ropes course in the first place, and I have just walked around behind the tree when I see it.

'Oh no!' I say.

Chelsea hears me and comes around. 'What is it?' she asks.

'It's a sugar glider,' I say. 'I think it's dead.'

By now, a small group of kids have gathered around. There on the ground is a beautiful glider. It's a soft grey colour with a dark stripe running down the centre of its head. Its beautiful dark round eyes are still open, but it isn't moving at all.

I crouch down to look at it more closely. Its little body is about the size of a small guinea pig and its tiny pink hands are curled in little fists.

'What could have happened?' says Chelsea. She sounds like she's going to cry. I feel like I might too.

'Aggghhh!' says Portia when she sees what we are gathered around. 'It's a dead rat!'

We all turn around and say 'Shhhh' to her at once. I think she gets the message.

Alex comes around to have a look.

'Ahh, that *is* a pity,' he says, gently lifting the glider for everyone to see. Its bushy tail is the same dark grey as its stripe, but it hangs lifelessly over the edge of his hand.

'There is no real way we could know what has happened to her,' he says. 'She probably died last night.'

All the kids stand and look at her for a long time. I think we all feel very sad to see something so beautiful that's not alive any more.

'Can we bury her?' I whisper to Mrs Hodby.

I know she's going to be worried about me touching it. 'I brought some gloves with me,' I quickly add.

'In her vet kit,' says Chelsea helpfully.

'That's funny,' smiles Mrs Hodby. 'I don't remember writing "vet kits" on the list of things to bring.'

She ruffles my hair and says it is okay with her as long as it is okay with Alex. He nods, and we all walk back towards the cabins.

CHAPTER
4

Vets need to be quiet sometimes

I race in, grab my kit and open it
on the bed. I have a few pairs of
disposable gloves from Mum's surgery,
so I put a pair on. I'm just about to
head back out when Portia comes in.

'Our cabin's not on washing-up duty
until tomorrow morning,' she says.

'We're going to bury the glider.'

'Oh, that's right,' she sneers. 'Mrs
Hodby chose you, because you're
nearly a vet.'

I ignore her and rush back to the

others. We walk down to a lovely spot by the creek. I hold the sugar glider gently while I wait for Chelsea and Maisy to dig a hole with some small shovels. I can't help but study her.

I look at her perfect little feet, her tiny pink nose and cupped ears. Sugar gliders are the softest animals I have ever touched. We had to raise some after a bushfire once, and I can't think of a single person who didn't think they were adorable. Even my dad liked them, and he's really not into animals that much – even though he is married to a vet!

I gently roll her onto her back and feel the soft folds of skin that join her front legs to her back legs. These are what she would have used to glide from tree to tree.

Suddenly, I see something that makes me catch my breath. I know straight away that we have a problem.

'I think she had a baby,' I say to the others. They stop digging and come and look. 'See, her teats and pouch are really stretched.'

I ask Chelsea to grab my Vet Diary out of my back pocket and turn to the pages on sugar gliders I wrote when we looked after them after the fire.

We look closely at my notes.

'The babies leave their mother's pouch when they are about 60 days old,' Maisy reads out loud. 'But they stay with them until they are seven to ten months old.'

We inspect the glider again. 'I think her baby would have still been with her if her pouch is still this stretched,' I say. 'We need to go back and have another look.'

We finish burying the mother and put some flowers on top of her little grave, and then we run back to the tree where she was found. We spend ages looking up, down and around the tree, but with no luck at all.

It's starting to get dark and Mr Thomson calls everyone over to start having their showers.

'I hope I'm wrong, and that she didn't have a baby with her,' I say, as we head back to our cabin. 'It won't be able to survive out there on its own.'

We have only been on camp for half a day, and already my shoes are filthy and my clothes have dirty marks all over them. The contents of my suitcase are all over my bed, with my kit in the middle of it.

Chelsea's shoes are still perfectly clean, her clothes are folded neatly in her case and her bed doesn't have a single thing on it, not even a wrinkle!

We grab our night-time clothes and head to the shower block. There is a long wait and Mrs Hodby starts banging on a couple of doors to tell people to hurry up in the showers.

Eventually a door opens and Portia steps out. Her hair is bundled up under a high towel wrapped around her head, and she is wearing little sandals and a flowery dress.

I look down at the tracksuit pants and T-shirt I'm holding. I know what I'd rather be wearing around a campfire!

'When you are out of the shower, head straight to the hall for dinner,' calls Mrs Hodby, and she heads off to check on who is still in their cabins.

Tiffany also comes out of the shower in a dress and sandals. She looks like she feels a bit silly about it.

'I just refuse to wear a tracksuit to dinner,' sniffs Portia.

'Oh, Tiffany, you're bleeding!' says Chelsea, pointing at her ankle. We all look down to see blood running down the back of her heel.

Portia screams, which makes Tiffany cry.

I bob down to look more closely. Above the blood, there is a shiny, black blob about the size of a jellybean hanging from Tiffany's leg.

'It's a leech,' I say. 'It's okay, Tiffany, it won't hurt you. I can fix this.'

'A leech! A leech!' Portia is still screaming and has now run out onto the verandah of the shower block.

Kids are coming from everywhere. Even the boys are pushing into the girls' showers, just so they can have a look.

Girls are crying, boys are gagging. The noise is deafening. We can hardly move. Tiffany looks like she is going to faint.

Mr Thomson blows his whistle. 'QUIET!' he bellows.

CHAPTER 5

Vets have to stay calm

Mr Thomson comes in to see what the problem is. He then makes everyone go outside, except the girls from our cabin.

Tiffany is really sobbing now. Chelsea and Maisy are holding her hands and patting her on the back. Portia is looking at herself in the mirror.

Mr Thomson looks down at the leech and the blood. I notice he starts to dab at his forehead with his hanky and looks a little pale. 'Um, you girls stay here,' he says. 'I'll just go and get the camp guide. He'll know what to do.'

'I know what to do,' I say.

Everyone stops and looks at me.

'I do,' I say. 'We have animals with leeches come into the surgery a lot.'

'She doesn't need a vet, she needs a doctor!' snaps Portia.

'She doesn't actually need a vet or a doctor,' I say.

'I'll go and find the camp guide,' says Mr Thomson. 'Sit down, Tiffany. I'll be back soon!'

'Be quick, because that thing is getting bigger!' says Portia, which sets poor Tiffany off again.

'Chelsea, I'm going to grab my kit,'
I whisper. She nods and I slip back to
our room.

I get back with it just before
Mr Thomson comes back in, with
Mrs Hodby following behind.

'We might just have to wait a little
while,' says Mrs Hodby, looking down
at the chubby black leech. 'Alex has
popped home for a while, and the office
is locked. We'll just sit here and wait
quietly.'

Tiffany has started wailing now.
'I want to go home. I want my mum.
Get if off! Get it off! Pleeease get it off!'

I open my Vet Diary to the page on
removing leeches that Mum helped me

with, and show the teachers. They both look at it with surprise and interest.

LEECHES

- Leeches are parasites, but they do not spread disease or cause pain

- Never remove a leech by putting anything on it, pulling it or burning it, as this will cause the leech to 'vomit' its stomach contents back into the wound before falling off, and this can cause infection

- To remove: tighten the surrounding skin gently, then flick it off using a fingernail or flat implement

- Treat the wound with antiseptic cream and cover with a bandage until the bleeding stops

'You have a whole page on leeches in your diary?' says Mr Thomson.

'I knew we were coming to a rainforest, so I wanted to be prepared,' I say, feeling a little bit self-conscious with Portia now pushing through the group to see the diary.

'Vets need to be prepared for everything,' adds Chelsea helpfully.

'Apparently, they do!' says Mr Thomson, smiling.

'My brother had a leech once, and Dad burnt it off with a match. Has anyone got any matches?' says Portia.

Tiffany starts crying again. Portia rolls her eyes.

'Well, Juliet's diary says not to do

that,' says Mrs Hodby. 'I think we might go with the information that she has, thanks Portia.'

'Do you feel confident doing this?' Mr Thomson asks me.

I nod my head firmly.

'Now Tiffany, this won't hurt at all,' I say. 'Do you know they actually put leeches on people and animals to make them feel better sometimes?'

'Yuck,' Portia says.

'They suck out all the bad blood and infection, and can be really useful,' I add. The whole time I'm talking I'm getting what I need from my kit. I have the perfect thing for flicking the leech off. It's the flat spatula that

Mum gave me for putting ointment
on things.

I pull the skin around the area
tight. Everyone is gathered around
the patient trying to get a closer look,
except Portia, who is now back in front
of the mirror. She isn't happy that the
teachers have listened to my idea.

Quickly and carefully I slip the very
thin flat end of the spatula towards
where the leech's head is attached to
Tiffany's leg. In one quick move I flick
it off. It flies across the bathroom.

'Get it off!' squeals Tiffany, her eyes
squeezed shut.

'It is off,' laughs Mrs Hodby. 'Our
vet has removed it, no trouble at all.'

'Thank you, Juliet,' says Tiffany very nicely, as I dab some antiseptic cream on the sore and quickly pop a pad and bandage over the small puncture mark on her leg. I make it nice and firm.

'Tiffany, leech bites can bleed quite a lot, but it's nothing to worry about. My mum told me that they have something in their saliva that stops the blood from thickening. It will settle down soon.'

'Where did the leech go?' asks Chelsea.

We all look around the room.

'It should stand out against the white tiles,' says Maisy.

'We'll need to put it somewhere

away from the cabins,' I say. 'It'll want to attach itself again pretty quickly.'

Everyone's looking really carefully now, except of course for Portia. She is sitting on a plastic chair looking rather impatient.

Suddenly Chelsea grabs my hand. I look at her. With wide eyes she nods in Portia's direction.

There, on her cheek, is a plump black leech.

She sees us looking at her and looks in the mirror before I have a chance to race over and get it off.

'AGGGHHHHHHH!' The scream is enough to freeze everyone in the entire camp mid-stride.

I race over with my spatula and flick it off her cheek before she has even taken another breath.

'It's off!' I have to yell at her to be heard.

CHAPTER
6

Vets need to be quiet sometimes

Even though it was Tiffany that
was actually bitten by the leech, the
conversation at dinner is all about
Portia. I overhear her telling the story
in the queue for dessert, and the way
she tells it, I flicked the leech at her on
purpose.

Tiffany comes to sit at our table to
eat her ice-cream and jelly. I think
she's a bit tired of hearing Portia's
silly stories too.

We sing songs around the campfire

and play a few games of 'statues' in the dark, which is really fun, then it's time to clean our teeth and go to bed. None of us look that tired, but Mrs Hodby and Mr Thomson do!

Portia is the first one into our cabin. Suddenly, the entire camp is frozen again by her ear-piercing scream. 'RAT!!!! There's a rat in our cabin.'

Mr Thomson is standing next to me. I hear him mutter something under his breath about not getting any sleep tonight.

Once again, everyone races to find out what is going on. But this time they are heading straight up the stairs to our cabin.

'It went under the bed. I saw it when I turned the lights on!' Portia cries. More sobs and wailing follow.

I'm not actually afraid of rats. I don't really understand why so many people are.

I slowly make my way up between the crowd on the stairs until I'm at the door of my cabin.

Mrs Hodby has also managed to push her way through.

'Where is it?' she asks, sounding a little less patient than usual.

Portia points inside at her bed. She is perched high up on the handrail outside.

'Can I take a look?' I ask Mrs Hodby.

'If you could, that would be wonderful, Juliet,' says Mrs Hodby.

Grabbing my torch, I get down onto my hands and knees. I shine the bright light into the dark corner underneath the bed. It certainly looks like a rat huddled in the corner, its face hidden from view.

But something about it makes me look twice. As quietly as I can, I slide forward on my stomach to get a better look.

'It's an antechinus!' I say cheerfully, more to myself than anyone else.

'An anti-what?' laughs Chelsea.

'An antechinus!' I say. 'They're amazing. They do look a lot like

rats, only a bit smaller, but the cool thing is that they are actually little marsupials! And, even better, this one has babies with her!'

I jump up and grab my Vet Diary. I'm sure I have a picture and some information about them in it. I find the page and show the teachers.

ANTECHINUS

- A small carnivorous (meat-eating) marsupial

- Eats cockroaches and other insects

- Has an open pouch, and the babies are dragged around under the mother for about 5 weeks

- Are often killed by people who think they are rats or mice

Mr Thomson lets all the kids creep in, two at a time, to have a quiet look under the bed and then at my diary page. Everyone is really interested in what I have written.

By the time they are finished, everyone wants an antechinus in their cabin!

'It probably came in looking for bugs to eat,' I say. 'If we leave the doorway clear, it will probably go back outside.'

Mr Thomson thinks this is a good idea. Together, we gently shoo the antechinus mother, with her babies hanging underneath her like little Christmas balls, back outside.

Eventually, Mr Thomson blows his

whistle hard and tells everyone that it's lights out and time for bed.

Some boys in the Carpet Snake cabin don't listen too well, but after a visit from both the teachers they seem to get the hint.

I think I'll have trouble getting to sleep, but even Portia's whispering and turning her torch on and off doesn't keep me awake, and I soon drift off.

CHAPTER 7

Vets need to listen as well as look

The next morning I wake up before it's even light. I'm not the only one awake. In fact, I can hear lots of kids slamming doors and running backwards and forwards to the toilets laughing and talking.

I hear another voice I recognise too. It's Mr Thomson. 'GO . . . BACK . . . TO . . . BED!' he bellows.

Everyone who wasn't awake is now.

While I am lying in bed, I can't help thinking about the baby sugar glider.

I hope I'm wrong, and that it had already grown big enough to leave its mother's pouch.

It's our turn to help get breakfast in the kitchen, so we are allowed to leave our cabin at 6am. The ladies in the kitchen are really nice, and it's our job to cook the toast, fill the cereal containers, stir the baked beans, set up the serving tables and put foil over the bacon and eggs to keep them hot. We even get to have breakfast before everyone else, because we have to help serve.

After breakfast and clean-up, our group heads over to the high ropes course. I arch my neck backwards to see the ropes in the tops of the trees.

'I don't think I can do this,' I say to Chelsea quietly.

'Yes you can, Juliet,' whispers Chelsea, squeezing my hand. 'You can't possibly fall. Just think, you'll get to see what possums and birds see.'

I smile. Chelsea always knows the right thing to say.

I am second last to have a go. Chelsea is last. Above me I can hear the excited calls as kids make their way along the ropes, switching their clips over at each section just like we've been shown.

Then, when they get to the platform at the end, another instructor, Chris, helps them into the flying fox for the very quick ride back to the ground.

'Woooo hoooo!' I hear the excited squeals of Maisy as she zips down from the treetops.

'Your turn, Juliet,' says Alex kindly from the platform above me. 'You'll be fine.'

'I'll be right behind you,' smiles Chelsea. They must be able to see that I'm a bit worried.

I slowly make my way up the ladder to the platform and hook my clips to the ropes like I've been shown. I can feel my knees shaking and my helmet is tight under my chin. My mouth is dry and my head feels funny.

'Keep going, Juliet!' I hear Chelsea call from below. 'Just pretend you are a sugar glider!'

But my arms won't seem to let go of the big tree. 'I think I want to get down,' I say to Alex.

I can hear Chelsea starting to climb the ladder behind me. I feel like

I'm trapped. The colour of the sun beaming through the trees and all the sounds of the other children are deafening as they swirl around me. I want to block them out. I close my eyes and hold my breath.

That's when I hear it for the first time.

Pshh, pshh, pshh, pshh.

My eyes fly open. I would know that sound anywhere. I heard it so many times when there was a fire and we rescued animals. There is no way it could be anything else.

It's the sound of a baby sugar glider calling for its mother.

'Stop!' I yell.

Chelsea and Alex are the only ones who stop. They look at me with puzzled faces.

'Did you hear that?' I say. We all strain to listen.

Nothing.

'What are we listening for?' asks Alex.

'A baby sugar glider. I heard a baby sugar glider!'

Alex looks a little confused. 'How do you know what a baby sugar glider sounds like?' he asks, a slight smile crossing his lips.

Chelsea has now made it to the platform too and stands with us.

'She knows, because she is nearly

a vet, for a start,' she says confidently.
'And we raised some baby native
animals after a bushfire, and Juliet
was in charge of the sugar gliders.'

'Oh,' says Alex. 'I see.'

We all stand quietly and listen
again. Still nothing – just the sound
of kids screaming and laughing down
below us.

I search the branches and trunk
desperately with my eyes.

Suddenly there is another sound
I recognise. Portia.

'Juliet's too scared to move,' she
announces to the group of kids who
have finished their turn and are now
gathered at the bottom of the tree,

looking up at our little huddled group.

'We think we can hear a baby sugar glider,' Chelsea calls down. 'Shh.'

Everyone goes really quiet. Except for one person. 'Oh, that's a good excuse, if ever I've heard one!' laughs Portia.

Chelsea is about to yell something back down at her, but I touch her arm.

'Don't bother,' I say.

'We really do have to keep moving. It's time to go back for morning tea,' says Alex gently. 'Perhaps it could have been a cicada?'

The look on my face must have told him otherwise.

'Hurry up, Juliet,' sneers the voice

from below. 'The other group will eat all of the cake.'

I look at Chelsea and shake my head. I'm not scared now. I am angry.

I reach out and grab the rope above me with all the confidence of Tarzan. I shuffle along without looking down. I clip my clips from one rope to the next without a stop, and sail down the flying fox without so much as a peep.

Before I realise it, I have reached the bottom. I thought it would feel like I was falling, but I felt like I was flying between the trees. It was actually great fun!

Then I march over to the group,

unclip my harness and plonk my
helmet into the box, glaring angrily
at Portia.

'Funny,' says Chelsea in a loud voice
for all to hear. 'Juliet didn't look too
scared to me!'

CHAPTER
8

Vets need to stand up for what they believe in

I don't feel like eating cake. Instead,
I go over to Mrs Hodby and ask her
if I can speak to her for a minute.
Chelsea comes with me.

I explain to her what I heard, and
she listens very carefully.

'Well,' she says, 'you've been right
about a lot of other animal things
on this camp, Juliet. I think it is
definitely worth another look. Give me
a minute.'

Mrs Hodby goes over to talk to Alex. We watch as he listens to what Mrs Hodby says. Chelsea and I have our fingers crossed behind our backs.

Then he stands up and heads away from the table.

Mrs Hodby comes back to us and says that we can wait for Alex behind the hall. He is grabbing his gear and he will climb the tree for another look.

I hug Mrs Hodby. I can't help it.

We quickly tell Maisy what's going on, and the three of us race back to our cabin and get my vet kit.

We meet Alex and Mrs Hodby behind the hall, and quietly head towards the tree where it all began.

We stand at the bottom of the tree in a quiet circle and listen. It's so much easier to hear, now that all the kids have cake in their mouths back in the hall.

Nothing.

Then . . . *Pshh, pshh, pshh, pshh.*

'Well, I'll be darned,' says Alex, and he fastens his harness with great enthusiasm. He looks at me and smiles. 'Our vet might be right again!'

He sweeps up the stairs of the ladder and waits silently on the platform.

Pshh, pshh, pshh, pshh.

Looking. Silence. More looking.

Pshh, pshh, pshh, pshh.

'There you are!' It's the words we've been holding our breath to hear.

Alex slips out a few metres onto the ropes and reaches to a thin branch. We can't see anything except his big hand wrapping around something small.

He slips it into his pocket, then slowly, slowly makes his way down the tree.

As we all gather around, he slides his hand into his pocket then slowly uncurls his fingers.

Ohhhhhhhh,' is all we can say. It is the most adorable baby we have ever seen.

I quickly open my vet kit and grab out one of the small, warm pouches

Chelsea's mum sewed for us during the bushfire.

'We've got to get her warm first,' I say, and Alex slips her gently into the pouch. Chelsea holds it against her chest so carefully it is like she thinks the baby is made of glass, while I rummage around to find what I'm looking for.

'Got it!' I say.

'What is it?' says Maisy.

'It's a little heat pack.'

I show them all the small packet with 'hand warmer' printed on the front.

'See,' I say, giving it a shake. 'People use these when they are skiing or in cold places to put in their pocket to keep their hands warm. Mum always has a few in her kit as they can be very handy if you need to keep something small heated. When you shake it, the chemicals in it mix and make it warm, but not too hot.'

I slide the now very warm little parcel in between Chelsea's hand and the outside of the pouch.

'You must never put the heat source right next to the animal. Always have some fabric between them.'

I see Mrs Hodby look over at Alex and smile.

'She is nearly a vet!' he says.

'So what should we do now?' asks

Maisy. 'We don't have any of the right milk for little mammals here.'

'We shouldn't feed her until she is warm anyway,' I say. 'We need to ring the closest vet, and they'll probably tell us how to contact a wildlife carer.'

'That would be Stan Miller,' says Alex. 'I have his number in my office. He picked up a wallaby for me that had been injured. He's a really great carer.'

Alex heads off to make the call.

Chelsea hands me the pouch and I cuddle it against my chest.

We slowly walk back towards the cabin. It would be far too noisy in the hall for this little baby.

Alex jogs back over a few minutes later to tell us the carer will be here in fifteen minutes.

The three of us sit on my bed and take it in turns to nurse the tiny, warm pouch. We don't open it to look in, as much as we all want to. This baby needs her sleep.

By the time the carer comes, Mrs Hodby and Mr Thomson have gathered everyone in the hall. The whole group has settled down and is sitting very quietly. We bring the little joey glider over.

The carer is waiting with the teachers. When he smiles at me, his warm grey eyes tell me that he will be

very kind to our baby, and that she is
going to be okay.

Fifty children hold their breath
as he slides his hand into the pouch
and brings out the tiny, grey ball to
examine her.

'Ahhhhhh,' is the only sound you
can hear.

Mr Millar tells the classes that
I have done everything right while
we waited for help to come. Everyone
smiles at me.

Then they smile up at him as he
explains the stages he will go through
now to help this baby survive and
eventually be released back into
the wild.

I whip out my diary and take some notes while he talks.

- Baby sugar gliders, like all marsupial babies, are called joeys

- At first she will spend most of her time in this pouch, and only come out for her little feeds of warm milk

- Sugar gliders like to live in a community, so she will be put in with two other little gliders already in care

- As she gets older she will want to explore more, so she will be put in a small cage, where she will still have bottles but will have solid foods like fruit, flowers and insects

- Then she and the other gliders will be put in a large aviary and eventually released as a group

I tell the wildlife carer that he can keep my little pouch and hand warmer, and he's very grateful.

All afternoon, whenever anyone sees me, all they want to do is talk about the rescue, and how cute the glider was.

That night, we all go spotlighting on a night walk. We see possums and owls and all kinds of night animals.

Best of all, we see a beautiful adult sugar glider gracefully gliding from the canopy of one tree down to another.

I hold my breath and hope that, one day, when she is grown, our baby will be able to do that too.

Then we finally make it to the glow-worm caves. The one we go into is about half as big as our classroom.

We turn our torches off once we are seated on little mats on the damp ground. As the darkness surrounds us, tiny specks of light begin to appear above us, like stars in a night sky.

It is very beautiful.

'You know, Chelsea,' I say when we are gathered outside the cave and are allowed to talk again, 'glow-worms are not actually worms.'

'Of course they're worms!' says Corey Smythe-Donnerly, rolling his eyes. 'Why else would they be called glow-worms?'

'Well, they're like mealworms,'
I say, shining my torch on my diary
to show the life cycle of a mealworm.
'They're just the larva stage of an
insect.'

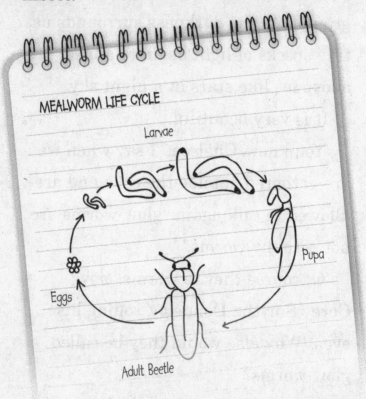

MEALWORM LIFE CYCLE

Larvae

Pupa

Adult Beetle

Eggs

Suddenly I hear a voice behind me
I know all too well.

'You'd better listen to her, Corey,'
says Portia. 'Juliet actually is nearly
a vet.'

Quiz! Are You Nearly a Vet?

1. **Brush turkeys lay their eggs in:**
   a. Burrows
   b. Mounds
   c. Nests
   d. Egg cartons

2. **Striped Marsh Frogs are:**
   a. Brown
   b. Green
   c. Rainbow coloured
   d. Yellow

3. **Sugar gliders are:**
   a. Birds
   b. Reptiles
   c. Mammals
   d. Amphibians

4. **To remove a leech you should:**
   a. Pull it off with your teeth
   b. Pull salt on it
   c. Burn it with a match
   d. Flick it off with a thin card or fingernail

5. **You should wear long socks hiking so that:**
   a. You don't get cold
   b. You look fabulous
   c. You don't get a leech
   d. People don't see your ankles

6. **The first thing to do when rescuing an animal is:**
a. Keep it warm and safe
b. Feed it something
c. Give everyone a hold
d. Take a selfie with it

7. **What is something teachers don't get to do on camp?**
a. Blow their whistle
b. Eat
c. Sleep
d. Sing

8. **Baby mammals must be fed on:**
a. Meat
b. Grass and vegetables
c. A mixture of honey and water
d. Special milk suitable for that mammal

9. **In a rainforest waterhole, you would not see:**
a. Sharks
b. Small fish
c. Turtles
d. Crayfish

10. **A glow-worm is a type of:**
a. Reptile
b. Worm
c. Insect
d. Fish

Answers : 1b, 2a, 3c, 4d, 5c, 6a, 7c, 8d, 9a, 10c.

The Great Pet Plan

My best friend Chelsea and I ♥ animals.
I have a dog Curly and two guinea pigs, but
we need more pets if I'm going to learn to be
a vet. Today, we had the best idea ever. . .
We're going to have a pet sleepover!

At the Show

Chelsea and I are helping our friend, Maisy,
get her pony ready for the local show. But
Midgie is more interested in eating than in
learning to jump (sigh). Pony training is a bit
more difficult than we thought!

Farm Friends

It's Spring and all the animals on Maisy's farm
are having babies. Maisy says I can stay for a
whole week and help out. There are chicks and
ducklings hatching, orphan lambs to feed, and
I can't wait for Bella to have her calf!

Bush Baby Rescue

A terrible bushfire has struck and Mum's
vet clinic is in chaos. Every day more injured
baby animals arrive. Chelsea and I have
never been so busy! But who knew that
babies needed so much feeding. I may never
sleep again!

Beach Buddies

It's the holidays and we're going camping by
the beach. I can't wait to toast marshmallows
by the campfire, swim in the sea and explore
the rock pools – there are so many amazing
animals at the beach.

Zookeeper for a Day

I've won a competition to be a zookeeper for a
day! My best friend Chelsea is coming too. I
can't wait to learn all about the zoo animals.
There will be meerkats, tigers and penguins
to feed. And maybe some zoo vets who need
some help (I won't forget my vet kit!).

The Lost Dogs

There was a huge storm last night and now there are lots of lost dogs. One turned up outside my window (he must have known I'm nearly a vet). Luckily, Chelsea, Mum and I are helping out at the Lost Dogs' Home.

Playground Pets

Chelsea and I have such a cool school – we get to have playground pets! Guinea pigs, lizards, fish and insects are all part of our science room. But this week, we have a replacement teacher, and Miss Fine doesn't know much about animals. Luckily we do (it's so handy being nearly a vet).

Outback Adventure

It's hot and dry in the outback where my grandparents live. I wonder what animals we'll see? My cousin Jarrod will be there, but I get the feeling he doesn't like me very much and – even worse – he doesn't seem to like animals! Maybe this is my chance to change his mind . . .

Cat Show Queen

There's a cat show in town and some of the cats are going to board at Mum's vet clinic. All the owners have special techniques for preparing their pets for the show – and some are very fussy. When there's a cat-astrophe, its lucky that my best friend is almost a world-famous animal trainer and groomer!

The Big Flood

It's been raining for days and the paddocks near our house are flooded. Luckily, Chelsea and I are ready to help – a vet has to be ready to go at a moment's notice! But there are many small animals that need rescuing. Can we convince Dad to take us out in the canoe before the water rises further?

From Rebecca Johnson

I've been on lots of school camps – first as a child
and then again as a teacher. I love going, because it
is always a chance to explore a new place and see
different animals. One night, we were in a rainforest
with a group of students and there was a full moon.
Sitting quietly on the grass together, we were lucky
enough to see a colony of little sugar gliders emerge
from a hole in a tree, one after the other, and glide
across the open space above us to reach a large gum
tree in flower. Juliet and Chelsea would have loved it!

From Kyla May

As a little girl, I always wanted to be a vet. I had
mice, guinea pigs, dogs, goldfish, sea snails, sea
monkeys and tadpoles as pets. I loved looking after
my friends' pets when they went on holidays, and
every Saturday I helped out at a pet store.
Now that I'm all grown up, I have the best job in
the world. I get to draw lots of animals for children's
books and for animated TV shows. In my studio
I have two dogs, Jed and Evie, and two cats,
Bosco and Kobe, who love to watch me draw.